Mystery of the
Thief in the
Night

Mystery
of the
Thief in the
Night

BY JANELLE DILLER
ILLUSTRATIONS BY ADAM TURNER

Published by WorldTrek Publishing

Copyright © 2014 by Pack-n-Go Girls

Printed in the USA

Visit our Web site at www.packngogirls.com.

This is a work of fiction. Names, characters, places, and incidents either are the product of the author's imagination or are used fictitiously. The town of Barra de Navidad, Mexico, is real, and it's a wonderful place to visit. Any other resemblance to actual events, locales, organizations, or persons, living or dead, is entirely coincidental and beyond the intent of either the author or the publisher.

Illustrations by Adam Turner

ISBN 978-1-936376-06-3

Cataloging-in-Publication Data available from the Library of Congress.

To Steve, my favorite traveling buddy. I can't wait for our next adventure.

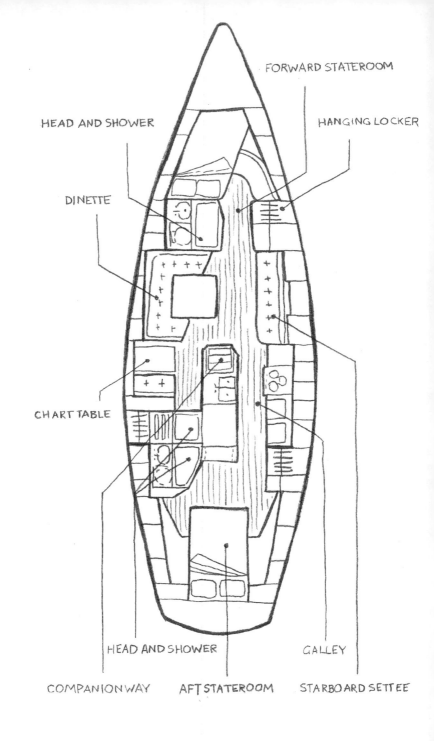

FORWARD STATEROOM

HEAD AND SHOWER

HANGING LOCKER

DINETTE

CHART TABLE

HEAD AND SHOWER

GALLEY

COMPANIONWAY

AFT STATEROOM

STARBOARD SETTEE

Contents

Meet the Characters

Izzy Bennett loves sailing to new places on Dream Catcher. Barra de Navidad is her new favorite anchorage.

Patti Cruz Delgado helps in the family restaurant. She's thrilled to have a new friend to play with.

Carlos Cruz Delgado is Patti's brother. He works for some fisherman when he's not working in the family restaurant.

Mr. Bennett

is Izzy's dad. He's always dreaming of taking his family sailing.

Mrs. Bennett

is Izzy's mom. She's having fun this year away from work while the family sails the coast of Mexico.

Senora Delgado de Cruz

is Patti's mom. She works long hours in the family restaurant and hotel.

The Thief in the Night
is out there somewhere!

And now, the mystery begins . . .

Mystery of the Thief in the Night

Chapter 1

Night Watch

Ka-BOOM!!

Izzy Bennett jumped a mile high.

Well, she didn't actually jump—and she certainly didn't jump a mile high—since she was sound asleep when the racket woke her. But her eyes flew wide open.

Katie Kitty, Izzy's cat, was the one who jumped a mile high. "Meowwwwww!" she screeched. She tumbled off the bed and leapt into the cubby below

Izzy's berth.

"Scaredy-cat," Izzy muttered. "We're just tacking." Her own heart pounded too, though, from the noise of the turn. She reached down into the cubby to scratch behind Katie Kitty's ears. It calmed both of them a bit. In a minute, the cat purred softly.

The water whooshed against the side of the sailboat. Izzy closed her eyes and tried to go back to sleep, but it wasn't going to happen. They were sailing in a direction that made the boat tilt at an angle. Izzy felt like she was going to roll off her bed.

When she slept at her grandma's house back in Seattle, she never had to worry about falling out of bed because the house leaned over.

There was nothing normal about life on a boat.

Izzy sighed and climbed out of her berth. She pulled on a sweatshirt and sweatpants and carefully made her way to the steps up to the cockpit. When they were at sea, it felt like they lived in one of those crazy circus funhouses. Nothing was flat. Everything was at an angle.

Her dad sat in the cockpit reading. She crawled up on the seat with him and snuggled close. He put his arm around her. "Izzy Lizzie. What are you doing up at two o'clock in the morning?"

"Katie Kitty woke me. She didn't like the noise from the tack." She didn't mention *she* didn't like the noise either. Izzy was always a little nervous at sea. Well, more than a little. But there wasn't any way to get their boat from one place to the next without going to sea. She tried not to think about all the scary things that could happen.

Like hitting another boat or even a whale.

Or being knocked over by a humongous wave and then sinking fast.

Or getting lost at sea.

Or, well, just about anything that meant she'd never see fourth grade.

She had a lonnnggggg list that got longer on every trip.

"Well, I'm glad to have a little company. Do you want to stand watch with me?"

"No," Izzy said. "But I'll sit watch with you."

Her dad laughed. "That's a good thing because I don't want to stand up and watch for other boats all night either."

"Why do we say we 'stand watch' when we're always sitting?" Izzy asked.

"I guess it's because hundreds of years ago boats didn't have a comfortable cockpit to sit in. People had to stand and look all around to see if there was land or another boat or weather that might be a problem."

"Or pirates?"

"Or pirates."

The two of them sat quietly for a few minutes. Izzy listened to the rush of the water against the boat. She wished she could see some dolphins swim by. Sometimes they did. She loved to watch them jump and flip beside the boat. But tonight she only saw the moonlight catch the waves.

Even though they were just off the coast of Mexico, it felt chilly. Nighttime on the ocean was always colder than it seemed like it should be. She pulled her knees up and stretched her sweatshirt over her legs. Her mom would say, "Izzy, don't stretch out your sweatshirt." But her mom was asleep, and it was so cozy like this.

"Izzy, can you keep an eye out? I'm going to go below and make some more coffee. Do you want some hot chocolate?"

"Yum! Can you put marshmallows in it too?"

Her dad disappeared down the steps. Izzy picked up the binoculars. She looked in all directions to see if she could see another boat. Just in case, she looked for pirate boats too. There hadn't been a pirate on the west coast of Mexico for over 100 years. But that didn't matter.

You could never be too careful.

Then she focused on the direction where land was. Tiny lights dotted the horizon. They looked as far away as the dots of stars in the sky.

Her dad climbed back into the cockpit. He handed her a mug of steaming hot chocolate.

"How much longer before we get there?" Izzy asked him.

"There" was Barra de Navidad. It was a favorite stopping point in Mexico for boaters, or cruisers. Izzy knew before they started their trip it would take over twenty-four hours of sailing to get to Barra, as everyone called it.

"Probably another eight or ten hours. It depends on the wind."

"What if the wind dies down?"

"Then we'll start the engine."

"What if the engine doesn't work?"

"Then we'll call on the radio for help from another boater."

"What if there aren't any other boats that can hear us?"

Izzy's dad laughed and put his arm around her. "What would you do if you didn't have something to worry about?"

Izzy thought a minute. "Well, I'd probably worry that I didn't have anything to worry about."

She slurped up a marshmallow and looked out at the night sky. Billions of stars twinkled in the black sky. She felt so cozy and warm next to her dad. For a few minutes she decided maybe she didn't have anything to worry about.

Except an asteroid hitting the earth.

Chapter 2

Welcome to the Lagoon

Fortunately, an asteroid didn't hit the earth.

Fortunately, too, by noon they were anchored in the quiet lagoon behind Barra de Navidad. Izzy had read about lagoons, but she'd never been in one before. This one was like a big lake with two islands. A wide sand bar separated the lagoon from the ocean. A narrow rock-lined channel connected the lagoon to the ocean. Izzy knew this meant the water would be a mix of salty seawater and fresh water.

This mix made the water brackish.

Low hills surrounded the water on three sides. A colorful village sat on the sand bar that separated the lagoon and the ocean. About 15 other boats shared the lagoon with them. Izzy hoped there would be another boat that had children to play with. Boating could be pretty lonely, even with Katie Kitty on board.

Izzy couldn't believe how flat the water was in the lagoon. Even with a little breeze blowing, there were no waves or swells. For the first time in what felt like forever, the boat sat perfectly level. Nothing creaked or clanked in the wind. Nothing groaned.

Izzy was going to like staying in the lagoon.

"Can we check to see if there's a kid boat?" Izzy asked.

"Sure thing." Her dad handed her the radio mike.

Izzy pulled out the script her mom had helped

her write. She pressed the button on the mike and read, "Attention in the fleet in Barra de Navidad. Attention in the fleet in Barra de Navidad. This is the sailing vessel Dream Catcher." She paused for a few seconds. She knew if there were children on any boats, they'd be listening. A kid's voice always got that kind of attention.

"We just arrived in the Barra Lagoon. We have one kid on board. Me! I'm Izzy, and I'm nine-years old. I have red hair and freckles, and I like to kayak. Are there any other kid boats here? Please come now."

"Please come now" was radio talk. It meant anyone else could get on the radio and respond. But in her head, Izzy really meant, "Please come over to my boat so we can play."

Izzy waited. And then she waited some more. But there was only silence.

She sighed. "Dream Catcher clear." That was the

signal she was done on the radio.

"Let's go explore the town," Izzy's mom said. "It's early afternoon. Maybe the other kids are done with their schoolwork and are off their boats."

Her dad lowered their rubber dinghy, Ringee Dingee, into the water. Izzy loved their little boat's name since "ding-ee" sounded just like "dinghy." Her dad said it was a play on words. Whatever that meant.

As Izzy and her mom were stepping into the small boat, a man in a ratty old dinghy puttered up to Dream Catcher.

"Afternoon." The guy tipped his faded red baseball cap at them. He stopped his engine so it got quiet. The man wore dark sunglasses and a stained white t-shirt without sleeves. A thick, curly blond fringe of hair stuck out from under his cap. He looked a little older than Izzy's dad, but it was always hard to tell with sailors since the sun aged people fast. For some reason, he gave Izzy the creeps. Then she realized it was because of the snake tattoo that started at his wrist and wrapped around his arm up to his shoulder. A shiny gold watch separated the snake's head from the rest of the snake.

She shuddered. She hated snakes.

"You just get into the lagoon?"

"Just in the last hour," Izzy's dad said. "We sailed down from Puerto Vallarta." Mr. Bennett stuck out

his hand. "I'm Mark and this is my wife, Annie, and our daughter, Izzy."

The other man shook Mr. Bennett's hand. "Pleased to meet you. I'm Skip. I'm over there on Lazy Dog." He pointed with his chin toward a tired looking boat. Izzy noticed it didn't even have any sails on it. She'd been sailing long enough to know there was a sad story that went with that boat.

"Nice to meet you, Skip," Mr. Bennett said.

"I pretty much live down here year 'round," Skip said. "Weathered the hurricane here last summer. Not a fun time. Ripped up my sails real bad."

"Sounds rough," Mrs. Bennett said.

"It was miserable. Your boat looks like it's in great shape. What is it? About a 42 footer?"

Mr. Bennett smiled broadly and Izzy sighed. She knew what was coming. Boat talk. There was nothing more boring, boring, boring than boat talk. Unless it was engine talk. That was even more boring, boring,

boring. She took off her hat and fanned herself.

Fortunately, Izzy's mom didn't like boat talk much more than Izzy. She cleared her throat, took off her own hat, and started fanning her face.

Mr. Bennett caught the cue. "Skip, it was nice to meet you. But we've got to head into town and get some lunch. If we don't, I might have a mutiny on my hands."

"Wouldn't want a revolt," Skip said and nodded at them. "Welcome to the lagoon." He pulled the cord to start his engine and zipped off toward town. His gold watch glinted in the noonday sun.

Chapter 3

One More Worry

The three of them motored to shore. Izzy studied
the other boats as they went by. She hoped to see
another kid or at least signs of them on board.
She looked for small swimming suits or laundry
hanging out to dry. Even a boogie board could be
a good sign. But she didn't see anyone or anything
that looked like a kid boat. If they had her
schedule, though, they were probably down below

in the boat doing schoolwork. Sometimes parents turned off the radio during schoolwork time.

Izzy sighed. She tried not to feel disappointed. She was lucky to spend this year on a boat.

Going to shore was the best part of sailing. Izzy loved the Mexican towns they'd been in so far. Many had cobblestone streets. They all had houses in rainbow colors: pink, blue, yellow, and green. It always looked to Izzy like the paint stores didn't even sell white paint.

Every town had little grocery stores, or *abarrotes*, that were no bigger than her grandma's living room. You could always find a sweet yellow pineapple or spicy green chili pepper. They might have a freezer full of colorful frozen popsicles. (Izzy loved the strawberry ones!) And they always had an ice chest with tortillas still warm from the local tortilla maker.

The best part of every town was the town square, or *plaza*. Shade trees and bushes bursting with colorful blooms made the plazas seem like small parks. People gathered there on the benches in the evenings when it was cooler. Kids always played there too. Sometimes, they invited Izzy to join them. Maybe she'd be lucky in Barra.

They motored up to a wooden dinghy dock, weathered grey from the sun and the sea. Izzy stepped up onto shore and tied off the boat. It looked like they'd come up to the back side of a small hotel. Palm trees and beach chairs surrounded a clear blue swimming pool. Between the pool and the hotel rooms were tiled paths crowded with flowers and bushes and more palm trees. It looked like a miniature plaza in the middle of the jungle.

"I'm starving!" Izzy's mom said.

"Well, it's a good thing there's a restaurant right here at the hotel." Izzy's dad led them to a table overlooking the water. The restaurant had no doors or windows. Instead, wide stone arches framed the two sides near the water. A wall hid the kitchen from the dining area. All the tables had cheery yellow and green tablecloths and yellow chairs. A young girl about Izzy's age brought them menus. A bright pink scrunchy held her long black hair in a loose ponytail.

"*Hola. Bienvenidos a Hotel Siesta Café,*" she said. She smiled big.

Hello. Welcome to Hotel Siesta Café. Izzy knew that much Spanish.

"What would you like to eat?" the girl said in English.

"You speak English?" It just popped out of Izzy's mouth. She hoped she didn't sound rude.

The girl nodded. "You are Americans, no? So I can practice English with you."

Izzy's mom laughed. "*Debemos practicar nuestro español.*" She looked at Izzy.

Izzy knew what she said. We should practice our Spanish. Izzy smiled at the girl and said, "*Por supuesto.*" It meant, "Of course." It wasn't exactly the right thing to say. But she wasn't sure how to say, "Yes, we should."

The young waitress laughed. "*¡Excelente!* You practice your Spanish with me. And I practice my English with you."

"Then you'll be doing all the talking," Izzy said. *"Mi español es terrible."* Izzy's Spanish *was* terrible. It was hard to learn a language from a book. She didn't get to practice enough even in Mexico.

Well, that wasn't exactly true. She had lots of chances to practice. But she didn't because she didn't want to be wrong. She hated sounding stupid.

"You must practice. I'll help you. My name is Patricia Cruz Delgado. Everyone calls me Patti. I am nine-years old. What is your name?"

"Izzy."

Patti tapped her pencil on the table like a teacher would. "No. You say it in Spanish."

One More Worry

Izzy felt shy, but she tried anyway. *"Me llamo Isabella Elizabeth Bennett. Pero todos me llaman Izzy. Yo tengo nueve años también."* My name is Isabella Elizabeth Bennett. But everyone calls me Izzy. I'm nine-years old too.

At least she thought that was pretty close. She wouldn't even try to say that her dad called her Izzy Lizzie for short. That would be way too complicated.

"*¡Perfecto!*" Patti clapped her hands and laughed. "See? It's easy. You have a very nice accent, Izzy. I can understand you."

"Where did you learn to speak English so well, Patti?" Mrs. Bennett asked.

"In school. And here. I get to practice all the time in the restaurant. My uncle lived in the U.S., so he helps me with it too."

Izzy liked this girl. She liked her easy laugh and her wide smile. She liked how friendly and helpful she was. All of a sudden, Izzy didn't care if there was a kid boat. She already had a new friend.

"I don't know how to say this in Spanish." She smiled and shrugged her shoulders. "Do you want to play with me this afternoon?"

"With you?" Patti got a funny look on her face.

Izzy felt silly. She realized Patti probably had tons of friends already. She wouldn't need a friend as much as Izzy did. "Uh, only if you have some time."

That sounded dumb.

"*Por supuesto.* Of course I would like to play with you." Her smile stretched across her face again. "No American girl has ever invited me to play."

Izzy knew she was never supposed to ask her mom about a play date in front of the other girl. But she knew her mom would understand. "Can Patti come to the boat and play this afternoon, Mom?"

"You're on a boat?" Patti's eyebrows flew up. She took a small step back.

For once, Izzy was glad she felt less worried than someone else. "It's okay. It's a very safe boat."

"The boat is in the lagoon?"

"Yes. The water is very flat. You won't even get seasick."

Patti shook her head. Her black ponytail swung a little. "You don't understand." She leaned in and whispered, "The lagoon is a very dangerous place now."

"What?" Izzy's heart sank. Just when she thought she didn't have anything to worry about.

"Very dangerous. Be very careful."

"Why? What's wrong?"

"There's a thief who steals things in the night."

Chapter 4

Carlos

"Patti, are you scaring off the tourists again?"

A teenage boy called to them from the other side of the room. He frowned and shook his head at her.

Patti shifted her eyes from the boy and back to Izzy's family. "That's my brother, Carlos," she said in her normal voice. And then she turned her back to him a bit so he couldn't see her face. She whispered, "It's true. I'll tell you more this afternoon."

The boy strolled over to the table. He brushed

his black hair out of his eyes and squeezed Patti's shoulder. He smiled at them. Something about it didn't look like a real smile to Izzy. She felt nervous.

"Patti likes to tell exciting stories, but don't worry. Everything is fine. You will be very safe in the lagoon." He said something to Patti in rapid Spanish that Izzy didn't understand. Patti looked like she might cry. She turned and ran into the kitchen.

"Please. What would you like to eat?" Carlos said.

Izzy didn't like this boy. He didn't need to be mean to his sister, especially in front of strangers. If she got to play at Patti's house someday, she hoped Carlos wouldn't be there.

The boy took their orders and disappeared into the kitchen.

Izzy's tummy felt all jumpy. She wanted to play with her new friend. But she didn't want to be anchored in a dangerous place.

"What are we going to do?" she asked her dad. She worried he would say they were going to pull up the anchor and leave. But she also worried he was going to say they were staying. She sighed. If only she could be nervous about one thing at a time.

"What do you mean, Izzy Lizzie?"

"Aren't you worried about the thief?" She looked at her mom and dad, who looked at each other. Her mom had that worried look too. Her eyebrows scrunched together a little. A small

wrinkle formed between them.

"I'm sure we'll be fine." That's the sort of thing her dad always said when Izzy worried. She didn't know if she believed him this time.

"But what if the thief comes aboard our boat while we're at lunch?"

"Well, maybe you'll be lucky and he'll steal your math book."

Izzy laughed a little, which helped. "But what if—" She stopped and took a deep breath. "What if he comes on board when *we're* on board?"

There. She'd finally said what scared her the most.

Her mom and dad looked at each other again. This time her dad got that little wrinkle between his eyebrows too. "Don't worry, Izzy Lizzie. We'll be safe." He patted her hand. "I promise."

She wished he sounded surer.

Chapter 5

The (Almost) Perfect Day

Mrs. Bennett and Señora Cruz took forever to set up the play date.

First they talked about the endless sunny weather.

Then they talked about the restaurant and the hotel Patti's family owned.

Then they discussed enchilada recipes.

After that, they talked about how there weren't as many tourists this year.

Then they found out Mrs. Bennett knew Señora Cruz's cousin who had moved to Seattle and worked in the same hospital as Mrs. Bennett. After that, they were new best friends. So after *that*, the two moms loved the idea their daughters could play together.

Moms worried too. Izzy knew that.

So that's how Izzy and Patti ended up splashing around in the hotel swimming pool. Mrs. Bennett and Señora Cruz had decided the girls should stay at the hotel and play instead of going out to Dream Catcher.

Izzy didn't care where Patti and she played. She only cared about having someone to hang out with. Besides, a swimming pool was a great place to spend a hot afternoon.

Izzy's dad headed back to the boat to clean it up from their trip to Barra. Izzy's mom stayed with Izzy at the hotel and read in the shade of a leafy palm tree. Patti's mom was just beyond that working in the

restaurant. From time to time, Izzy spotted Carlos'
black, wavy hair as he waited on customers.

Mrs. Bennett gave the girls some pesos to dive
for. All afternoon, they threw the Mexican coins
in the water and raced each other to pick them up.
Every time they came up for air, they laughed like
crazy.

This was exactly the kind of day Izzy had been
missing.

Finally, the girls paddled over to the steps and
rested. Patti's mom brought them two icy orange
sodas, a small bowl of tortilla chips, and a dish of
spicy *pico de gallo* to dip the chips into. Sailing life
NEVER got better than this.

"Do you know what *pico de gallo* means?" Patti
asked.

Izzy shrugged her shoulders. "Isn't that the
Spanish name for salsa?"

"Yes, but if you translate it directly from Spanish

to English, it means beak of the rooster."

"What? You put rooster beaks in the salsa?" Izzy stopped dipping her chip.

"No, silly. That's just what we call it. A rooster's beak is sharp. I guess the salsa tastes sharp too."

"That still seems like a funny thing to call salsa."

"Well, when you eat cotton candy are you really eating cotton that's turned into candy? Or when you eat a hot dog, are you eating a dog that's hot?"

Izzy laughed. She'd never thought about words like that before.

The girls scooped up the last of the salsa. Izzy took a long swallow of soda to cool her tongue. "So is Hotel Siesta your house?" she asked.

Patti nodded. "We live up there." She pointed with her chip to the second floor above the restaurant. A covered balcony ran the length of the L-shaped hotel. Izzy counted twelve shiny wooden doors on the second floor and eight doors on the first floor. Ruby red flowers climbed up the lemon yellow stucco walls. The bright splashes of color and the tidy jungle around the pool gave Izzy a happy feeling.

"Do you live in hotel rooms?" Izzy thought that would be a little strange. She guessed it would be okay, though, as long as she could stay in the same room as her mom and dad.

"Kind of. When my grandfather built the hotel, he made those rooms like a little apartment." Patti glanced at the restaurant. "My brother Carlos has a hotel room next door to ours."

"He doesn't live with you?"

"Well, the apartment space isn't very big." Patti shrugged her shoulders. "And the hotel has plenty of extra rooms these days." She glanced around the nearly empty swimming pool and patio. "Even most of the people here are people from the boats in the lagoon. If they buy lunch or even just a soda, my mom and dad let them spend the afternoon here."

"But why?" Izzy asked. "This is such a pretty hotel. It's so clean and your family is very friendly." Well, except for Carlos, Izzy thought. But she didn't say it out loud.

"I know," Patti said. "When I was little, all the rooms were full and the restaurant was so busy my mom couldn't sit to rest for five minutes." She shook her head. "Now? There's no one." For the second time that day, it looked like Patti might cry.

"Where are the tourists? Why aren't they coming here anymore?"

Patti shrugged her shoulders. "My dad says people don't have as much money to spend on vacations. And when they do, they want to go to big fancy resorts. Not quiet little towns like Barra de Navidad."

"Well, they're missing something. I'd much rather be here than anchored near some city. That's how most boaters feel too." Even as Izzy said it, though, she remembered how empty the lagoon was compared to other anchorages.

Patti must have been thinking the same thing. She rested her elbows on her knees and her chin on her fists. "There used to be 50 or 60 boats in the lagoon this time of year. Now how many are there? Ten? Fifteen?"

"Sixteen. With us." Izzy looked at her friend. "But why? The lagoon is beautiful and flat. It's the best anchorage we've been in."

Patti looked over at the restaurant. Señora Cruz sat at a table and fanned herself. Carlos was nowhere to be seen. She turned back to Izzy and whispered, "It's because of the thief. That's why all the boaters have stopped coming to Barra. They're scared."

Even though the sun baked down on her shoulders and the water felt as warm as a bathtub, Izzy suddenly had goosebumps.

Chapter 6

The No-win Decision

"But are we safe here?" Izzy asked her dad for the third time. The three of them were sitting in the cockpit of Dream Catcher eating fish tacos, Izzy's favorite. The whole western sky burst with sunset colors. Brilliant oranges, reds, and pinks painted the clouds.

Mr. Bennett put down his taco and wiped his mouth with his napkin. "Well, Izzy, I talked to a couple of other boaters today. They said the thief is stealing dinghies. So far, he hasn't taken anything else."

"So far," Izzy repeated. "What does that mean? That everyone expects it to get worse?" She looked at her mom and dad. "Are we safe here?"

All she wanted was a yes or no answer so she'd know how much to worry.

Izzy had already fallen in love with this place. She couldn't imagine a sweeter

spot to stay for the next several weeks—unless she was scared every night because of a thief.

After all, she did like to sleep.

"We're safe, Izzy." Her dad reached across the table and squeezed her shoulder. "I won't make any promises about Ringee Dingee, though." He laughed, like it was some kind of a joke.

"It's not funny, Dad." She crossed her arms and huffed a little.

"I know it's not, Izzy Lizzie. But we'll haul the dinghy up out of the water every night. We'll lock it to the boat the best we can." He helped himself to another fish taco and sprinkled some chopped cabbage on it. "Trust me, I don't want to lose Ringee Dingee any more than you do."

Now that was one more thing for Izzy to worry about. She'd only thought about how scary it would be to have someone steal Ringee Dingee. She hadn't thought at all about how hard it would be without a boat to take them to shore. If they lost Ringee Dingee, they'd be stuck in marinas or would have to spend some of their precious boating money on another dinghy. Either way, they'd run out of money earlier. They would be forced to stop sailing much sooner than they'd planned.

Suddenly, it made things a lot worse.

"Do you want to leave Barra de Navidad, Izzy?" her mom asked.

Her mom and dad always let her be part of the decision of when to leave an anchorage. She was really lucky since most kids just had to go wherever their parents wanted to go, even if they were having a terrific time with other kid boats.

Izzy felt miserable. If they stayed, she'd be scared and worried. If they left, she knew she'd be sad to leave even after just a single day here. She and Patti had had the best afternoon ever. She hated to leave her new friend and this pretty little town. She was the one who felt like crying now.

Her mom gave her a quick hug. "We're not going anywhere tonight. Ringee Dingee is up and safe, so we're fine. We'll make a better decision in the morning after we've all rested."

Izzy nodded. She began to clear the dishes off the table. That was always her job. Then she helped her mom or dad do the dishes.

"Honey, you've had a big day. I know you're tired from swimming all afternoon," her mom said. "I'll do the dishes tonight. You get ready for bed. I know you want to get your schoolwork done in the morning so you can go play with Patti again tomorrow."

Izzy brushed her teeth and put on her pajamas. She kissed her mom and dad goodnight and crawled into bed. Katie Kitty jumped up onto Izzy's berth. She squeezed between Izzy and the boat hull, her usual cozy place. Izzy scratched the cat behind her ears. They both felt better. Moments later, Katie Kitty purred contentedly.

Izzy wanted to spend some more time worrying about everything. But she fell asleep halfway through that thought.

Chapter 7

The Familiar Fisherman

PLOP, PLOP, Plop, plop, *plop, plop, plop, plop, plop,*
plop, plop, plop, plop.

"OH, NO! Ringee Dingee!" Izzy panicked. She
popped her head out of her stateroom hatch. A
second later, she realized that was a dangerous and
stupid thing to do.

The dinghy still hung off the back of the boat.
Whew!

Izzy looked around for the source of the weird

sound. The first hint of peachy sunrise color lined the horizon. From Dream Catcher to the edge of the lagoon, the water was completely calm. It would be a perfect morning to kayak across the glassy surface. She stretched and breathed in the cool morning air.

PLOP, PLOP, Plop, plop, *plop, plop, plop, plop, plop, plop, plop, plop, plop.*

There it was again. This time, it was closer. It sounded like a very short rain. But Izzy knew it wasn't rain.

She climbed out of her hatch and crept over to the other side of the boat. Her feet left footprints on the dewy boat deck.

PLOP, PLOP, Plop, plop, *plop, plop, plop, plop, plop, plop, plop, plop, plop.*

A fishing *panga* floated near Dream Catcher. It looked like it had a couple of buckets. A tarp covered the bow, or front, of the boat. Izzy could

make out the shape of two men in the boat. One
man rowed. The other man stood up and threw out a
large circular net. When the edges hit the water, they
plop, plop, plopped.

"*Buenos días, Señorita,*" the fisherman said softly.
"*¿Qué haces tan temprano?*" What are you doing up so
early?

"*Buenos días, Señor.* You're up early too." She
watched the man pull up the net. A couple of small
fish caught in the net wiggled. The man pulled the
fish out and dropped them in a bucket.

"Good bait for the big fish out in the ocean, *sí?*"

"*Sí. Buena suerte.*" Good luck.

The *panga* floated quietly by Dream Catcher. Just like a ghost.

As they passed by, Izzy got a good look at the teenage boy rowing the boat. Carlos Cruz Delgado looked up at her and gave a tiny hello nod.

Chapter 8

The Thief Strikes!

Izzy flew through her schoolwork that morning. Patti would be done with school at 1:00.

Izzy thought Mexican schoolchildren were lucky to get out of school so early. When Izzy told her that the day before, Patti had shaken her head no. "I have to be in school at 7:30 in the morning. After I leave school, another group of kids start their school day in the same classroom with the same teacher. It makes the teachers a little grumpy because they're so tired," Patti had told her. "I'm just glad I get to go in the morning instead of the afternoon."

The two girls were meeting at the pool again today. Izzy couldn't wait to see her new friend.

"I think you're in a teensy bit too much of a hurry with your schoolwork, Izzy Lizzie," Mrs. Bennett said. "It's hours before you meet Patti. You might as well get your math right the first time. Or it'll take you even longer."

Izzy sighed, but she went through her math problems again. She found SIX mistakes. Ugh.

While she worked, the morning radio net for boaters came on. In popular anchorages, boaters checked in with each other every day and shared information. They gave weather and tide reports. They also shared news and helped each other out with problems. Most mornings, Izzy only half listened when the net was on.

She moved on to her spelling words.

The Thief Strikes

"Good morning. This is Nancy on the sailing vessel Moon Dance."

Izzy perked up. She knew Moon Dance from another anchorage. It was nice to hear a familiar voice and have a face to go with it. She liked Nancy, partly because she always made great brownies for the cruiser potlucks.

"Let's listen for any emergencies," Nancy continued.

Almost always, there was just a bit of silence since there were rarely any emergencies. This time an angry voice broke in.

"Lazy Dog."

"Yes, Lazy Dog. Go ahead."

Izzy looked at her dad. "That was the boater we met yesterday when we got here."

He nodded and dialed up the volume.

"I just want to tell the fleet that my dinghy was stolen last night. Whoever stole it, cut the lines. I slept through the whole thing." The man paused for just a moment. "Those local fishermen are getting bolder!"

Izzy twitched. Carlos and the other guy. Were they really fishing? What was under the tarp in their boat? Tools to cut ropes and padlocks?

"Lazy Dog," Nancy said. "We need to be careful about jumping to conclusions. We don't know if the fishermen are stealing the boats."

"And you didn't just get your dinghy stolen," he fired back. "This is the second one this week."

Izzy's stomach turned upside down. She couldn't concentrate on spelling anymore.

The rest of the morning passed in a fog. Izzy somehow got her schoolwork done. She was pretty sure, though, she didn't learn anything that would stick in her brain. The whole time she felt like she had a knife poking at her stomach from the inside out.

The Thief Strikes

Over lunch, the only thing they talked about was whether to stay or leave. Mrs. Bennett leaned toward leaving. Mr. Bennett preferred staying. And Izzy was too miserable with either choice to help decide. Her dad was pretty sure he could tie down Ringee Dingee with enough chain so a thief wouldn't try to steal it. In the end, that tipped the balance.

Finally, they finished the lunch dishes and climbed in Ringee Dingee. Izzy patted the rubber sides. She had a new appreciation for their little boat. Without it, they would have to pay a water taxi to come get them and to take them back to the boat. That got expensive. Expensive meant they had less money for sailing. Less money meant a shorter time to live on the boat.

Izzy patted the rubber boat again.

They pulled up to the dinghy dock just as Patti arrived home from school. She was dressed in a crisp white shirt and a blue and orange plaid skirt. She'd

pulled her hair back with a blue and white scrunchy. Izzy knew that school children in Mexico usually wore uniforms. In other towns, she'd seen packs of school children walking together on their way to or from school. All dressed the same like that, they somehow reminded her of pretty flocks of birds.

"*Hola, amiga,*" Patti said.

Hello, friend.

Izzy liked the sound of that. "*¡Hola, amiga!*"

Patti smiled cheerfully and shifted her backpack to her other shoulder. "I'm going to eat a quick lunch. Then I'll come to the pool and we can play."

Izzy and her parents settled in by the pool. Her dad drifted over to chat with another boater. Izzy only heard bits and pieces of what they were saying, but she knew they were talking about the boat theft. It worried everyone.

Izzy waited patiently for Patti. Lunch seemed to be taking a long time. She finally decided to head over to the restaurant. Maybe she could sit with her while she ate.

She stepped into the cool shade of the restaurant. Almost immediately, she realized her mistake. The place was empty except for Patti, Carlos, and Señora Cruz. Patti looked ready to cry. Carlos stood facing his mom. His fists were on his hips. A shiny gold watch stood out on his brown skin. His jaw jutted

out. His eyes were squeezed into thin black lines.

Only Señora Cruz talked. Izzy couldn't understand a word she said. But she understood the finger pointing and the speed of the words. Señora Cruz was very angry about something.

Izzy backed away quickly. But it was too late. Carlos spotted her first. He jerked his chin in her direction. Señora Cruz turned toward her. Her shoulders drooped and she sighed.

"I'm sorry, Señora Cruz. I just came to find Patti. I'll wait by the pool."

"Is okay, Izzy. We're done here." She turned back to Carlos and put her hand out to him, palm up. Carlos said something. Again, Izzy couldn't understand it, but he sounded very angry. He put something into Señora Cruz's hand and then stomped away. A minute later a door above them slammed.

Patti burst into tears.

Chapter 9

The Plan

When Patti finally made it to the pool, she still looked sad. She also didn't feel much like playing.

The two girls sat on the pool steps. Izzy leaned back on her elbows. She gently kicked a bit in the water.

"I'm sorry, Patti. I should have stayed by the pool and waited for you."

Patti shook her head. "It's okay." She looked close to tears again. "Well, it's really not okay."

The Plan

"What's going on?" Izzy asked. Her mom
would have told her it was none of her business. But
she hated to see her new friend so sad.

Patti sighed. "Sometimes, my brother Carlos
goes out with a fisherman who takes tourists fishing.
The fisherman pays him a bit and he usually gets
tips from the tourists. Today, he came back with
a huge tip. He said they caught a giant tuna. The
tourists were thrilled."

"But why was your mom so mad? I would think
she'd be very happy."

Patti shook her head. Her eyes grew wet, and
a tear rolled down her cheek. She looked at the
restaurant and up at Carlos' door. She turned back
to Izzy and whispered, "You know that another
dinghy got stolen last night?"

Izzy nodded. She didn't think she'd like what
Patti would say next.

She was right.

"My mom thinks Carlos is helping steal the boats. She thinks the 'tip' was his share of the stolen boat."

Izzy's felt sick. "I don't know how to tell you this, Patti. I woke up early this morning when I heard the fishermen casting for bait. Carlos was in that boat. There was something under a tarp in their boat."

Patti's eyes grew big. "Do you think he could have done it?"

"I don't know. He was in the lagoon."

"But others could have been there earlier."

Izzy nodded. For Patti's sake, she hoped it wasn't Carlos. "Patti," Izzy said and then stopped. She didn't know how to ask this question. She knew she had to ask it though. "Patti, do you think Carlos could be one of the thieves?"

"No! Carlos would never steal from others. He works very hard for the fisherman. And then he comes back and works in the restaurant. He's really tired when he does that. But he wants to help the family." She shook her head firmly. "His dream is to take over the hotel and restaurant some day. Like my mom and dad did from my grandparents. He wants it to be a busy, happy place. He would never steal boats since that drives away the boaters."

"I believe you, Patti." Izzy did believe her. "Then we have to prove he's not a thief."

"But how can we do that?"

The two girls sat in silence. Izzy scooted off the step and floated in the pool. She ducked her head under and dove to the bottom. The cool water cleared her thinking a bit. She paddled back to the steps.

"I have an idea," she whispered to Patti. "It's a long shot, but it just might work."

Chapter 10

Midnight Watch

It was easy to get Mrs. Bennett to let Patti spend the night on the boat.

It was a little harder to convince Señora Cruz. She was in a bad mood about Carlos, and she wasn't sure the lagoon was safe. But in the end, she agreed.

Patti invited Izzy up to their apartment while she packed. The simple, two-room space had a bedroom for Patti's parents and a living area with a worn foldout couch for Patti to sleep on. Dressers and various bookcases and cabinets lined the wall with family photos on all of them. A newer looking TV sat in a corner. Izzy could understand why Carlos lived in the hotel room next door. Everything was tidy and clean, but there wasn't much room for three people. Four would have been crazy crowded.

Patti took her schoolbooks out of her bag and put in her pajamas, toothbrush, and clothes for Saturday. She also put in her favorite doll, a soft one with shiny black hair and big brown eyes.

The girls got into Ringee Dingee with Izzy's parents. They puttered off to the lagoon.

When they got to Dream Catcher, Mr. Bennett helped everyone off. Then he raised Ringee Dingee onto Dream Catcher's deck.

Izzy was excited to give Patti a tour of the boat. They started in her stateroom. Izzy introduced Patti to Katie Kitty. She showed her the head, or bathroom, and how complicated it was to use. She explained how to pump the handle and then turn the lever on the toilet. And then you had to pump the handle again a gazillion times and then turn the lever one more time and pump it a whole bunch more.

Patti agreed. It was complicated.

Finally, Izzy showed her the galley, or kitchen. They had the most amazing galley of any boat their size. It had tons of storage and enough counter space that Izzy could help her mom roll out the dough for cinnamon rolls.

Their freezer could even make ice and keep ice cream cold.

Patti stayed strangely quiet through the whole tour.

"Are you feeling a little seasick, Patti?" Izzy knew that people sometimes felt a little queasy with the boat motion.

"No, I'm fine. Really," Patti said.

"Is everything okay?"

"Sure. I'm fine," Patti said. She paused for a moment and then went on. "You must be really rich to live on this boat. Your parents don't work. How can you do this?"

Izzy was confused for a moment. They lived on a budget. They couldn't stay in marinas very often. And they rarely ate out. They weren't poor. She knew that. But she never thought of her family as rich either. Izzy thought of all the things they did to save money for this year away and how many years they'd been saving. They never ate out in Seattle. And her dad's friends teased him because of the old car they drove.

Izzy knew it was all worth it now, though.

Then she thought back to the tiny space Patti lived in. Their boat, though small, was still bigger than Patti's apartment. Izzy knew how lucky she was to have her own stateroom, even if it was teeny tiny.

"We're not rich, Patti. My mom and dad bought this boat before I was born. This was always our house. Before we started sailing, we lived in a marina in Seattle. I'm really lucky to be able to do this. My mom's a nurse and my dad is an architect. They had to plan a long time ahead with their managers to take this year off of work."

"It's different in every country, isn't it?" Patti said. "My uncle lived in California. He tells stories sometimes about how different it is there."

"It is different. That's one of the things I feel

lucky about, I guess. I get to know what it's like to live in the U.S. And I get to see what it's like to live in Mexico."

Patti smiled. "And I get to know a little about the U.S. because I know you."

"We're both lucky."

"Girls," Mrs. Bennett called at that moment. "Dinner is ready."

Mrs. Bennett had grilled chicken and baked potatoes. She'd also made a lettuce and tomato salad. Patti ate it all very quickly. Izzy was relieved. It was a meal that was familiar to Americans and Mexicans.

The girls cleared the dishes and helped Mr. Bennett wash and dry them. When they finished, Izzy asked her dad, "Can we sleep in the cockpit tonight?"

Mr. Bennett gave her a funny look. "You're not scared? After all the worrying about the dinghy thefts?"

Izzy shook her head. It wasn't exactly true, but if she and Patti didn't sleep in the cockpit, well, the plan wouldn't work.

Her dad looked at her mom. Her mom shrugged her shoulders.

"Well, if you want to. I suppose you can. Let's get the cushions set up and get out some blankets."

"Can we pull back the bimini too? We want to see the stars."

Her dad pulled back the cockpit shade. The entire sky opened up above them. This was the very best part of living on a boat.

"And can we use the star app on your phone?"

Mr. Bennett pulled the phone out of his pocket and set up the star app. Now the girls could point the phone to the sky and see the names of the stars and constellations. It was like having a special window into another world.

"I'll pull the bimini back over you when I go to

bed," Mr. Bennett said. "You don't want to wake up wet and chilly from the dew."

The two girls explored the moonless sky. They showed their dolls the stars too. They talked about which of the constellations Izzy could see from Seattle. It was fun to think that wherever Dream Catcher went, Izzy and Patti would see the same stars.

Some time later, Izzy woke up just enough to hear her dad pull the bimini back over the cockpit. She fell back to sleep again before he was down the steps into the boat.

Chapter 11

The Thief Disappears

A gentle buzz woke Izzy.

"Patti," Izzy whispered. "Patti, wake up. The phone alarm went off. It's 1:00 in the morning."

Patti rolled over. She blinked her eyes and then shut them again.

"Patti." Izzy gently shook her friend. "Wake up."

Patti yawned and blinked her eyes again. This time, though, she sat up and rubbed her eyes.

Izzy had no idea if this crazy plan would work.

They were going to stand watch together. Only instead of looking out for other boats on the open water, they were going to watch boats in the lagoon.

There were two big problems with the plan.

First, they would have to stay awake.

And second, even if they did, there was no guarantee the dinghy thief would come tonight.

Crazy. Impossible. Nearly hopeless.

But maybe, maybe, maybe, it could work. After all, it was a new moon. Wouldn't a thief want the darkest night of the month to work?

Izzy crept below to the salon, their living room on the boat. Her dad snored softly just a few feet away. Very quietly she picked up the binoculars.

By the time she got back to the cockpit, Patti was curled up sleeping again.

"Patti!" She shook her friend. "This is our only chance to prove that Carlos isn't a thief. We have to stay awake."

The Thief Disappears

Patti sat up again. She wrapped the blanket around her. The two girls took turns looking around the lagoon. Slowly, they woke up a little more.

It was crazy. All Izzy's life she'd worried about stuff that wasn't ever going to happen. Finally, now that something *could* happen, she felt surprisingly calm.

A light breeze blew in the lagoon. All the boats had drifted around and pointed straight into the wind. From the sky, they would have looked perfectly lined up. Each one would be parallel to the others.

Dream Catcher sat near the back of the fleet. Only Lazy Dog sat behind them. They had a good view of the sterns, or back ends, of all the boats. That's where most people kept their dinghies.

Now they just had to be patient. And they had to hope tonight would be the night another dinghy would be stolen.

The girls whispered about all the things little girls talk about when they're trying to stay awake at a slumber party. And this was the most important kind of slumber party.

They told stories about their best friends and their worst enemies. It was kind of funny to Izzy. Patti's stories sounded a lot like Izzy's. The two girls realized that girls are the same around the world.

Katie Kitty finally found the girls in the cockpit. She jumped up on the cushions, and they took turns petting her. She purred and purred. Katie Kitty couldn't have been happier.

By 2:00, nothing had happened. Izzy really wanted to just lie down again and go to sleep. Patti poked her. "Stay awake, Izzy!"

They decided they would only speak Spanish for 15 minutes. Izzy was surprised she knew so many words. She even understood Patti, mostly because Patti talked slowly and used simple words.

"You should try harder, Izzy," Patti said. "Your Spanish is really good."

The Thief Disappears

"Your English is so much better."

"Only because I'm not afraid to make mistakes. Don't be afraid, Izzy. What's the worst that could happen?"

In a funny way, that was the smartest thing anyone had ever said to her. What's the worst that could happen? She always worried about the worst that never, ever happened. It meant she worried about so many things instead of looking for the good things that could happen.

"Shhhh. *¡Mira!*" Patti said.

Look.

On the other side of the anchorage, a *panga* glided into the lagoon.

Izzy raised the binoculars. "I see two people."

She handed the binoculars to Patti.

Patti nodded her head. "Two people."

The girls looked at each other. "This could be it," Izzy said. Her heart pounded.

The *panga* drifted quietly from one boat to another. Finally, it stopped at a boat just up from Dream Catcher.

Two men stood up in the *panga*. Izzy couldn't see what they were doing, but she knew it wasn't anything right. She pulled out her dad's phone and snapped a picture. A quick check told her that nothing showed up.

The Thief Disappears

"I have to get my dad."

Patti nodded.

"Go," she said. "I'll watch them."

Izzy tumbled down the steps. "Dad! Dad! Someone's stealing a dinghy!"

Her dad's snoring turned into a couple of quick breaths.

"What?"

"Come up! Someone is stealing a dinghy!"

She climbed back up the steps as fast as she could.

"It's down in the water," Patti said.

She heard her dad fumble around below. Izzy took another photo and then another. And another. The *punga* towing a dinghy drifted past them and into the black water beyond. Izzy kept snapping pictures.

Mr. Bennett popped up into the cockpit. "Where are they?"

"They're gone," Izzy said. "They drifted off over there." She pointed into the darkness.

"That doesn't make sense. Why would they go deeper into the lagoon? They must have gone around the island and headed back out to the channel and out to sea."

He dropped back down in the salon and turned on the radio.

"Attention in the fleet in Barra de Navidad. Attention in the fleet in Barra de Navidad. The thieves have just stolen another dinghy. They're headed around the island and out the channel. If anyone can hear this, come now."

Silence followed.

Mr. Bennett switched channels to the water taxi channel. He explained about the dinghy theft in a jumble of English and Spanish.

Patti climbed down the steps. "Let me help," she said.

Mr. Bennett pressed the mike key. Patti explained in Spanish what had happened. The water taxi service said they'd go out into the channel and stop the thieves from taking the dinghy out to sea.

"There should be plenty of time to catch them," Mr. Bennett said. "You girls have done a brave thing tonight."

Mrs. Bennett came out into the salon in her nightgown. She made hot chocolate for all of them while the girls told their wild story.

"You took pictures?" Mr. Bennett asked.

They scrolled through the photos on the phone. Mostly, they were black shadows on black water. The thieves had black hoods and black T-shirts. They blended into the dark water around them.

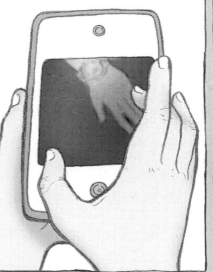

"Wait," Izzy said. "What's this?" It looked like something shiny.

They spread the photo wider on the phone.

"It's a watch, isn't it?" Mrs. Bennett said.

"It's a gold watch," Izzy said. She looked at Patti.

The two of them nodded sadly at each other. They both knew who had a gold watch. It was Patti who finally spoke. "Carlos."

Chapter 12

Snakes, Spiders, and Crocodiles

Forever later, the water taxi called back. They spoke briefly with Patti.

"No one ever came through the channel," she said.

Izzy wasn't sure if that made Patti happy or sad. Either way, there was no good ending to this.

"Nothing more is going to happen tonight, girls," Mrs. Bennett said. "Let's all try to get a little sleep. We'll sort it out in the morning."

Izzy didn't think she'd ever fall asleep. But Katie Kitty crawled onto the cushion with her. She scratched her behind the ears. Before Katie Kitty could even start purring, Izzy fell asleep.

Izzy woke up when the first rosy colors of dawn lined the sky. She tried to go back to sleep, but she couldn't. It didn't make sense that the *panga* and dinghy could just disappear like that.

She sat up and wrapped her blanket around her. She stared out at the empty lagoon behind the fleet.

The water lay so perfectly flat. It looked like a giant mirror as it caught the early morning colors.

Izzy didn't know much about lagoons. But the water had to come from somewhere besides the sea. Otherwise, it would be all salty water, not brackish water.

Izzy heard her mom in the galley below. She was up and making coffee. In a bit, Izzy would smell the rich scent.

"Patti." She nudged her friend. "Patti, where does the fresh water come into the lagoon?"

"Huh?" Patti rolled over.

"Do you want to go kayaking?"

"*¿Ahorita?*" This minute?

"*Sí. Ahorita.*" Yes. This minute.

Patti sat up and rubbed her eyes. "I'm sure you have a good reason to go before breakfast."

"Maybe."

The girls put on shorts and sweatshirts and zipped into life jackets. Mr. Bennett lowered the kayak onto the water and helped them climb in. He handed them a handheld radio and paddles.

"Have you ever kayaked?" Izzy asked Patti.

"*Claro que no.*" Of course not. Patti said it with a smile in her voice.

"No problem. It's really easy. Sit and get comfortable." She let Patti get settled. "You can stretch your legs out. Just dip your paddle in when I dip my paddle in. There's no wind or water current. It shouldn't take much work."

The two girls pushed their way through the water toward the back of the lagoon. They glided past Lazy Dog. Skip sat out on deck. As they passed, he called to them. "Where do you girls think you're going? Don't you know there are crocodiles in the lagoon?"

Crocodiles?

Izzy sighed. One more thing to add to her never-ending list of things to worry about. It was as long as her arm and growing.

Patti whispered to her. "Don't worry. They aren't very big."

"WHAT?"

"It's a joke, Izzy. I think he's trying to scare us."

"Well, it's not hard to do." Izzy paddled harder.

A very light fog lay on the water. Izzy knew that happened when the air was cooler than the water. It didn't matter what she knew, though. The mist *felt* spooky. The trees at the edge of the lagoon looked like milky white ghosts surrounding the water.

The girls glided closer to the mangroves that lined the lagoon. Snowy egrets filled outer edges of the trees. The birds squawked and cooed to each other and the girls as they paddled past.

"What are we looking for, Izzy?

"I don't know. Is there a stream that runs into the lagoon?"

"I think there's one over there." She pointed with her paddle. "I've never been this far into the lagoon."

"Really?"

"There's no reason to go."

"Well now there is. What could be a better place to hide a dinghy than someplace no one goes?"

Izzy took long, deep strokes with her paddle. Patti was helping too. They didn't go as fast as she did with her mom or dad, but they still scooted over the water to the far side of the lagoon.

"There." Patti pointed again. "That's the *estuario*. I don't know the word in English. But that's where the water comes into the lagoon."

Izzy was surprised. "It's almost the same. The word is 'estuary' in English."

They glided to a break in the mangroves. Immediately it grew darker with the growth around and above them. The mist grew thicker in the cool shade.

Mangrove branches made an arch over the estuary. Roots dangled from branches. They looked like long snakes reaching down to the water. With the low tide, the mangrove roots at the foot of the trees spread out like spiders.

Snakes and spiders. And maybe crocodiles. All of them scared Izzy. And now they were kayaking into the heart of them.

Birds and shadows of birds fluttered past them. Izzy tried not to think about bats. Of course, that

only made her think about bats. She wished she had worn a hat.

The estuary narrowed into a stream that twisted and turned. Crabs scuttled along the roots. Their legs clacked against the branches. Out of the corner of Izzy's eye, they looked like gigantic spiders running sideways.

The girls could still hear the snowy egrets calling to each other. Their cooing echoed softly through the trees. Deep in the mangroves like they were, the birds sounded uneasy.

It gave Izzy goosebumps.

Something splashed a few feet away. Both girls jumped.

"Do you think we should turn around?" Patti whispered. She sounded as scared as Izzy felt.

"No kidding. Let's get out of here." Izzy shuddered. "This place gives me the creeps."

"How can we turn around? It's so narrow."

Snakes, Spiders, and Crocodiles

Izzy felt a little sick. "I don't know. We'll have to paddle farther to find a place that's wide enough." She was sorry she'd ever come up with this crazy idea.

The mangroves grew tighter. The girls had to duck their heads so the dangling roots didn't hit them. Each paddle stroke took them deeper up the stream.

"What if a spider or snake drops on us?" Izzy asked.

Patti shuddered. "What if we're reaching the end, and we have to turn the kayak around?"

"The kayak is light," Izzy said. "It's just that we'd have to—" she paused.

"We'd have to get in the water," Patty finished what Izzy didn't want to say. "What do you think is in there?"

"Snakes and crocodiles."

"And crabs," Patti said. "Big ones that pinch hard."

"Thank goodness spiders don't go in the water," Izzy said.

"At least that we know about."

"Don't say that." Izzy stared at the water, but it was too dark to see anything.

Something jumped and splashed just behind the kayak. Patti squealed and turned to look.

"Patti, watch out!" Izzy shouted. A low branch nearly hit Patti's head.

The girls ducked.

They slipped under the branch. Their hearts pounded.

Izzy stopped paddling. The kayak drifted forward. "This is too scary. How can we get out of here?"

"I don't know. I don't think we have a choice. We have to keep following the stream till we can turn around."

Izzy took a few deep breaths. She dipped her

paddle in again and they floated forward. The trees began to thin a bit. It even looked like a small sunny patch and some rocks ahead.

When they passed the rocks, they were close enough to touch a small family of turtles sunning themselves.

"Crocodiles and snakes—"

"Don't say it," Izzy interrupted her. She'd already thought about how reptiles like warm rocks.

"Look." Izzy pointed her paddle up ahead. "There's a bend. It looks like we should be able to turn around there."

The stream grew slightly wider at the bend. Izzy paddled on the right side of the kayak then dipped the paddle on the left side. Holding the paddle in the water worked like a brake. The kayak shifted around and pointed in the direction they'd come. She stroked again.

Patti said. "What was that?"

Izzy shuddered. Snakes, spiders, and crocodiles. She paddled faster.

"No. Wait! Stop, Izzy!"

"What?"

"In that wide spot back there. Stop the kayak."

Izzy dropped her paddle in the water. She had to trust Patti.

"Can we back up?" Patti asked.

Izzy paddled backward a couple of strokes. She shifted the kayak toward the wide spot.

"Look!"

Ahead of them three grey ghosts floated silently on the water.

"The stolen dinghies!"

The girls laughed in relief. "We did it. We found them," Izzy said.

"We've got to radio your mom and dad."

Izzy pressed the "talk" button on the handheld radio. "Dream Catcher, Dream Catch—" The radio BEEP beeped.

"Oh no," Izzy groaned.

"What's the matter?" Patti asked.

"Dad grabbed the wrong radio. The battery is dead on this one."

The girls looked at each other and at the dinghies.

Izzy sighed. "Let's get paddling."

Chapter 13

Catching the Thief

"We found the dinghies!" Izzy shouted to her dad. They were still a few feet away from their boat. In the early morning calm, her voice carried across the still water.

Heads poked out of boats. Several people cheered.

Izzy tied off the kayak and climbed aboard Dream Catcher.

"What happened? Where are the dinghies? Why didn't you tell us what you were doing?" The questions flew.

Izzy and Patti told the quick version.

"You're just in time for the morning net," Mr. Bennett said. "We'll tell the fleet and sort out what boats are there later." He turned on the radio. Moments later the net started.

"Good morning. This is Nancy on the sailing vessel Moon Dance."

Good, Izzy thought. Nancy was running the net again.

"Let's all listen for any emergencies," Nancy continued.

Mr. Bennett smiled at the girls. Before he could speak, another boat broke in.

"Lazy Dog."

"Lazy Dog. Come now."

"Yes. I just wanted the fleet in Barra to know that I found the stolen dinghies last night."

The girls looked at each other and at Mr. and Mrs. Bennett. They were confused. They were disappointed too. It would have been especially fun to be the ones to tell the rest of the fleet.

"The dinghies stolen from boats in the lagoon?" Nancy asked.

Lazy Dog came back. "Yes. I was exploring the lagoon yesterday evening in my kayak. I found three dinghies up the estuary. I believe these are the boats stolen from the lagoon. It looks like whoever stole them was storing them there. They must have been waiting to sell the boats and the motors."

"That's wonderful news, Lazy Dog," Nancy said.

"I'm sure some fishermen are the thieves," he added.

"We don't know that yet," Nancy said. "We're glad you at least found the boats."

The net continued with check-ins and the usual information.

Mrs. Bennett dished out fresh fruit and breakfast burritos. The four of them ate in silence. Even Katie Kitty seemed quiet.

Catching the Thief

"You know," Izzy began. "What doesn't make sense to me is that Skip on Lazy Dog said he found three boats. But the last boat was stolen in the middle of the night."

"You're right," Patti said. "Shouldn't he have said he found two boats?"

The four of them looked at each other.

"I think we've just figured out who the thief is," Izzy said. "Only the thief would know there were three boats in the estuary."

"But wasn't his dinghy stolen too?" Mr. Bennett asked. "If he was the thief, why would he steal his own boat?"

"Maybe he was just trying to keep people from thinking he's the thief," Patti said.

"Maybe," Mr. Bennett said. "I think we're going to need more proof than we have."

The four of them sat in glum silence.

"Wait a minute," Izzy said. "Dad, can I see your phone?"

Mr. Bennett pulled the phone out of his pocket. Izzy touched the photo icon and tapped on the last photo. She spread it big enough to see the gold watch on the thief's arm. And then she spread it a bit bigger.

"Look. Do you see what's on his arm?"

"I see the gold watch," Patti said. "But plenty of people have gold watches. Including my brother." She sighed.

"Look again." Izzy traced her finger up the man's arm. "You can barely see it. It's a long tattoo."

"Like a snake," Patti said.

Izzy nodded. "Just like the snake tattoo on Skip."

Chapter 14

No More Worries

Skip on Lazy Dog was arrested by 11:00 that morning. It didn't take long for him to admit he'd stolen the boats so he could sell them. He even admitted that he'd "stolen" his own boat so no one would suspect him.

"I ran out of money. Then my sailboat engine quit working and I had no way to fix it," he told the police. "Stealing dinghies and selling them seemed like the simplest solution to get some money to fix my engine."

He also told the police who had helped him. Sadly, it *was* a local fisherman. Fortunately, it was *not* Carlos.

"This is the best anchorage ever!" Izzy said when they all finally sat down to lunch in the cockpit. "It's beautiful and calm. And I have a new best friend."

"I do too," Patti said.

"And now we're safe," Izzy said. "Best of all, I'm not worried."

Katie Kitty jumped on her lap and purred.

Sneak peek of the next book

Mystery of the Golden Temple

Chapter One

Jessica Johnson knew the drill. Shoes off. Jacket off. No water. Put your bag on the moving belt-thingee. And don't forget to give them your favorite stuffed puppy, Pink Dog. It didn't matter that her favorite stuffed animal had been through the moving belt machine-thingee a gazillion times, Jess still worried a little. What if THIS time she didn't come out on the other end?

The officer motioned Jess to step through the metal arch. He glanced up at the top. "Step aside and wait here, please." The man smiled and nodded in the direction he wanted her to go. She already knew she needed to wait for her mom. It was all part of the drill.

Jess fidgeted with her favorite soccer ball necklace while she waited. She craned her neck to see the other end of the moving belt thingee. Pink fluff crushed up against someone else's suitcase at the end. Now she had to worry that someone would see how cute Pink Dog was and take her. No one ever did, but what if THIS time someone did?

Airport security? A major drag.

Thank goodness her mom stepped through the arch at that moment. They gathered their stuff off the belt-thingee. Jess grabbed Pink Dog and hugged her big time.

This trip was the farthest away from home Jess had ever been. Her mom had showed her Thailand on their globe. She couldn't believe it was on the other side of the planet. Her mom said they'd see golden palaces and temples and jungles. They might even get to see some elephants.

Jess couldn't stop wondering about so many things. "Are the people in Thailand nice?" she asked her mom. "Do they speak English? Do I have to eat anything weird?"

"Jess, the food in another country is not 'weird.' It's just different from ours. Don't worry about it. You'll be just fine," Mrs. Johnson said.

Just fine. Oh yeah. Jess had heard that one about a million times. In her nine short years, Jess had been "just fine" in over ten different countries already. And it wasn't always "just fine."

Like the time they bought the wrong tickets for the ferry in Greece. They had to sleep all night on hard benches instead of cushy seats.

Not just fine.

Or the time it took ten hours to go 200 miles on a winding, dusty road in Peru.

Definitely NOT just fine.

Find out what happens to
Jess and Nong May in the next
Pack-n-Go Girls book,
Mystery of the Golden Temple.

Coming Soon. . .

Dive into More Reading Fun with Izzy and Patti!

Mystery of the Disappearing Dolphin
It's market day in Barra de Navidad. Izzy and Patti discover a beautiful glass dolphin that Izzy wants more than anything. Unfortunately, it disappears before she can buy it. Even more unfortunate? It later reappears in Izzy's bag. Izzy can't believe the trouble she's in.

Mystery of the Not So Empty Room
Patti invites Izzy to a quinceañera party and Izzy is beyond excited! As they get closer to the special day, though, things start to fall apart. First, Patti's brother, Carlos, disappears. And then a room that's supposed to be empty is anything but.

Meet More Pack-n-Go Girls!

Discover Thailand with Jess and Nong May!
Mystery of the Golden Temple
Nong May and her family have had a lot of
bad luck lately. When nine-year-old Jess
arrives in Thailand and accidentally breaks
a special family treasure, it seems to only
get worse. It turns out the treasure holds
a secret that could change things forever.

Discover Austria with Brooke and Eva!
Mystery of the Ballerina Ghost
Nine-year-old Brooke Mason is headed
to Austria. She'll stay in Schloss Mueller,
an ancient Austrian castle. Eva, the girl
who lives in Schloss Mueller, is thrilled
to meet Brooke. Unfortunately, the
castle's ghost isn't quite so happy.

Don't miss the second Austria book, *Mystery of the Secret Room*.
Coming soon, the third Austria book: *Mystery at the Christmas Market*.

What to Know Before You Go!

Where is Mexico?

Mexico is the country that borders the United States to the
south. Don't be confused, though. It may be south of the US,
but it's still part of North America. The country is shaped like
a funnel with a long, thin finger on the western edge. At the
top, it's wide and runs from Texas to California—almost 2,000
miles. At the southern end, it's about 700 miles wide. It shares
borders with Guatemala and Belize. Mexico has 31 states and a
Federal District, which is like our District of Columbia.

Facts about Mexico

Official Name: United Mexican States

Capital: Mexico City, which is in the Federal District

Currency: Peso

Government: Mexico became a country in 1917. It is a representative, democratic, and republican form of government.

Language: Spanish

Population: 117,409,830 (as of 2013 estimate)

Major Cities:
- Mexico City: 8,851,080
- Ecatepec de Morelos: 1,688,258
- Guadalajara: 1,564,514
- Puebla: 1,539,819

Traveling in Mexico

Most Americans fly into resort cities in Mexico. Another option is to drive. The road system isn't as easy as it is in the United States, so it's a good idea to drive during the daylight and not at night. When you drive, you get a better sense of what the country is really like. You see the small towns, the farms, and the people going to work. Mexicans are usually very courteous to people from other countries.

What to Expect for Weather

If you go to a coastal town, it will be warm and comfortable most of the year. If you travel through the interior, it's more mountainous and chilly. It can even snow in the winter. Further south, it's warm in the winter and hot and humid in the summer.

What Mexicans Eat

Americans think of Mexican food as spicy. It may be depending on the region, but you can always find food that isn't spicy. Regardless, Mexican food is full of flavor. Many pepper flavors, from mild to spicy and fresh to roasted, are common. It's easy to find something good to eat. Tacos, quesadillas, and burritos are everywhere. So are hamburgers, french fries, and grilled chicken. Fresh, homemade tortillas make every meal yummy.

Recipe for Pico de Gallo

This recipe is best when it's fresh. Be sure to get an adult to help you sauté the garlic and chop everything else.

Ingredients:

- 1 large clove garlic, peeled, chopped, and sautéed
- 4 plum tomatoes, finely chopped
- 1 small white onion, finely chopped
- ½ cup cilantro
- 2 jalapeno peppers, seeded and finely chopped [Be sure to wash your hands with soap after you've chopped the peppers. Otherwise, if you touch your eyes or nose, they'll sting from the pepper juices.]
- juice of 1 small lime
- 1/2 teaspoon salt

Combine all the ingredients and serve with crispy tortilla chips.

Say It in Spanish!

English	Spanish	Spanish Pronunciation
Hello	Hola	OH-la
Good day	Buenos días	BWEH-nohs DEE-ahs
Good afternoon	Buenos tardes	BWEH-nohs TAR-dehs
Good evening/good night	Buenos noches	BWEH-nohs NOH-chehs
Goodbye	Adiós	ah-DEE-OHS
See you later	Hasta luego	Ah-sta loo-A-go
Please	Por favor	poor fah-VOR
Thank you	Gracias	GRAH-see-ahs
Excuse me	Perdone	pehr-DOHN-eh
You're welcome	De nada	DAY NAH-dah
I'm sorry	Lo siento	low see-EN-toh
Yes	Sí	SEE
No	No	NOH
When	Cuándo	KWAHN-doh
Where	Dónde	DOHN-deh
Why	Por qué	por keh
What	Qué	keh
Who	Quién	kee-EN
How	Cómo	KOH-mo

English	Spanish	Spanish Pronunciation
Excellent	Excelente	Ex-ceh-LEN-teh
Welcome	Bienvenidos	Bee-EN-veh-NEED-thos
Of course	Por supuesto	Por soo-PWES-to
My name is ___.	Me llamo ___.	Meh YAH-mo ___.
I am ___ years old.	Yo tengo ___ anos.	Yo tehn-go ___ AHN-njos.
Fishing boat	Panga	PAHN-gah
How are you?	¿Como estas?	KOH-mo es-TAHS?
Good luck	Buena suerte	BWEH-nah swer-teh
0	cero	SEH-roh
1	uno	oo-noh
2	dos	dohs
3	tres	trehs
4	cuatro	KWAH-troh
5	cinco	SEEN-koh
6	seis	SEH-ees
7	siete	see-EH-the
8	ocho	OH-choh
9	nueve	noo-EH-beh
10	diez	dee-EHS

My Mexican Trip Planner

Where to go: _____

_____

_____

_____

_____

_____

_____

_____

_____

_____

_____

_____

_____

What to do: _____

My Mexican Trip Planner

_____

_____

_____

_____

_____

_____

_____

_____

_____

_____

_____

_____

_____

113

My Mexican Trip Planner

Things I want to pack:

_____

_____

_____

_____

_____

_____

_____

_____

_____

_____

_____

_____

_____

_____

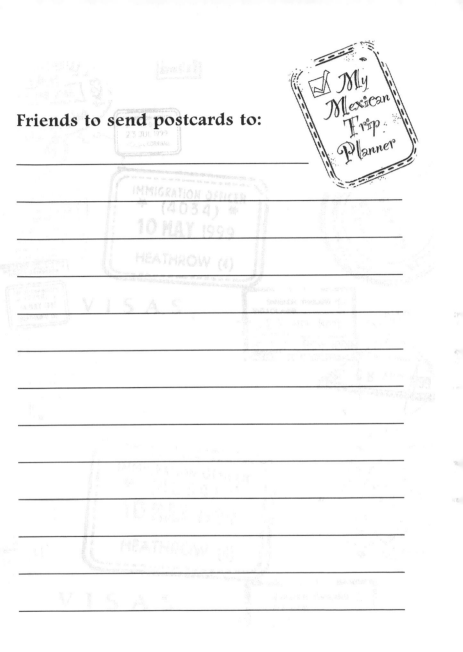

Friends to send postcards to:

My Mexican Trip Planner

_____

_____

_____

_____

_____

_____

_____

_____

_____

_____

_____

_____

Thank you to the following Pack-n-Go Girls:

Anna Allen
Maia Caprice
Elizabeth Moore
Meredith Rainhart
Abby Rice
Skylar Stanley
Sarah Travis
Emma Webb

Thank you also to Linda Bello-Ruiz, Kate Bridgman, Susan Grover, Linda Hackman, Jeannie Sheeks, and Patricia Castillo Villaseñor.

And a special thanks to my Pack-n-Go Girls co-founder, Lisa Travis, and our husbands, Steve Diller and Rich Travis, who have been along with us on this adventure.

Janelle Diller has always had a passion for writing. As a young child, she wouldn't leave home without a pad and pencil just in case her novel hit her and she had to scribble it down quickly. She eventually learned good writing takes a lot more time and effort than this. Fortunately, she still loves to write. She's especially lucky because she also loves to travel. She's explored over 45 countries for work and play and can't wait to land in the next new country. It doesn't get any better than writing stories about traveling. She and her husband split their time between a sailboat in Mexico and a house in Colorado.

Adam Turner has been working as a freelance illustrator since 1987. He has illustrated coloring books, puzzle books, magazine articles, game packaging, and children's books. He's loved to draw ever since he picked up his first pencil as a toddler. Instead of doing the usual two-year-old thing of chewing on it or poking his eye out  with it, he actually put it on paper and thus began the journey. Adam also loves to travel and has had some crazy adventures. He's swum with crocodiles in the Zambizi, jumped out of a perfectly good airplane, and even fished for piranha in the Amazon. It's a good thing drawing relaxes his nerves! Adam lives in St. Paul, Minnesota, with his wife and their daughter.

Pack-n-Go Girls Online

Dying to know when the next Pack-n-Go Girls book will be out? Want to learn more Spanish? Trying to figure out what to pack for your next trip? Looking for cool family travel tips? And teachers, interested in some complimentary learning resources to use while your students are reading *Mystery of the Thief in the Night*?

- Check out our website: **www.packngogirls.com**
- Follow us on Twitter: **@packngogirls**
- Like us on Facebook: **facebook.com/packngogirls**

Made in the USA
San Bernardino, CA
15 December 2014